Cathy Warren

Saturday Belongs to Sara

Pictures by DyAnne DiSalvo-Ryan

Bradbury Press • New York

10   9   8   7   6   5   4   3   2   1

The text of this book is set in 15 pt. ITC Zapf International Medium.

Library of Congress Cataloging-in-Publication Data. Warren, Cathy. Saturday belongs to Sara.   Summary: Sara and her mother set aside Saturday as a special day to spend time together doing the things they enjoy most.   [1. Mothers and daughters— Fiction]   I. DiSalvo-Ryan, DyAnne, ill.   II. Title.   PZ7.W2514Sat 1988 [E]   87-11783   ISBN 0-02-792491-2

For my friend Connie Mele—C.W.

For Susan and Janet—D.D.-R.

M OM says Saturday will be a "no watch" day. We won't worry about what time it is or what we have to do next. We will spend the whole day together at Dolphin Bay, just the two of us.

"Annie's had her special day," Mom told me. "Tomorrow is for you, Sara."

"Hooray, it's Saturday!" I cried to Annie, when I woke up this morning. She pretended she didn't hear me and went on practicing her flute.

Secretly, I have been hoping for a day like today for a long time. But something always happens to surprise me, like my mom's unexpected business trips or my big sister's music recitals.

I love to listen to Annie play. I like the way the notes sound crisp and clear. Sometimes, I beg her to let me try a note, but she always says, "It's much too difficult for someone your age."

Around my house, everyone is always rushing. I'm known for being the slow one. Annie says I'm lazy and calls me slowpoke. Mom just laughs and says I have a different sense of time.

Usually, I like to wake up gradually, but this morning I jumped out of bed. I was dressed and down the stairs before eight.

"You're up early," Mom said. "Let's see, it's Saturday," she said, teasing. "Is something special happening today?"

"Mom!" I cried.

We had danish and hot tea and talked about the weather, just the two of us.

"They say there's a chance of rain," Mom said.

"It looks perfect to me," I said. The sun was shining in patches on the kitchen table.

"Then let's get busy," said Mom.

I got out the bread while Mom climbed up on the kitchen cabinet and pulled down the picnic basket.

"It's been too long since I've seen you, my friend!" she said to the basket.

Sometimes Mom likes to talk to things that can't talk back, especially when she's happy or in a silly mood.

I made cheese sandwiches, one for each of us and an extra one, just in case. I felt happy and a little silly too, so I put a jar of olives and a box of toothpicks into the basket.

"Why those?" asked Mom.

"Appetizers," I said, laughing.

"You goof," she said.

Then we both giggled.

We were loading the basket into the back seat of the car when my aunt drove up. She's my mom's sister and her name is Claire, but Mom always calls her Sis. She has blonde hair and green eyes. Annie looks a little like her. I look more like Mom.

I'm usually excited to see her. She always has a surprise up her sleeve. Once last summer, she took us river rafting. Last winter, she taught us to ice skate. Mom says aunts are good for things like that. But today, I wasn't in the mood for surprises.

"Hello!" she called out, holding up two tickets.

"They're for the symphony," she said. "Doesn't that sound like fun?" She turned to me.

"Well . . . ," I said. I looked at Mom and hoped she wouldn't change her mind about our day together. All of a sudden, the day seemed kind of dark, and I could see Dolphin Bay shrinking until it almost disappeared.

"Oh, they're not for you," said Aunt Claire, when she saw the look on my face. "I know all about your special day. I'm taking Annie!"

I jumped into the car quickly, before anything else unexpected happened.

"Would you do a small favor for me, though?" Aunt Claire asked Mom. "My dear friend Mrs. Ivey lives all alone in a house near Dolphin Bay and has broken her ankle. Would you visit her?"

"This Saturday belongs to Sara," Mom said. "She'll have to decide."

I didn't feel like sharing Mom, not today—and not with a stranger.

"If you ask her, she might play the clarinet," added Aunt Claire.

"Well, all right, we'll go." I said.

"Wonderful," she cried, clapping her hands together.

She gave Mom directions to Mrs. Ivey's house. I pretended I wasn't listening, but I was—and carefully. Around my house, Mom is known for getting lost. Aunt Claire says she doesn't pay attention. I think she has a different sense of direction.

Annie was waving from our bedroom window as we pulled out of the driveway. A gentle breeze was blowing. We drove past the houses in our neighborhood. No one was out yet but the birds. They were singing loudly. The sun was twinkling through the green elm leaves and turning them golden.

Soon, we were on the road that led to Dolphin Bay. We passed a graveyard for old cars and trucks and a gas station. I peeked at the gas gauge, just in case.

"Shall I turn on the air-conditioning?" asked Mom.

"I like the fresh air better," I said.

"So do I," said Mom.

We rolled the windows all the way down. The wind picked up Mom's long brown hair and lifted it up and back. I shook my hair, which is shorter but the same color as Mom's, so I would look just like her.

We came to a field of wildflowers. There were goldenrod, Indian paintbrushes, and bluebonnets.

"Those bluebonnets are such a pretty blue," said Mom.

"They look purple to me," I said.

They are Annie's favorite. Any other time I might have asked Mom to stop so I could pick some for her. But, I thought, today is my day and I don't have to share it.

Then we came to another field of low green plants that seemed to have something red hidden in them.

"What are those?" I asked.

"Strawberries," Mom answered.

I love strawberries, but we hardly ever have them. Annie is allergic to them. She gets all itchy whenever she eats them. Sometimes at the grocery store I beg Mom to buy them. "I'm sorry, just having them around the kitchen is too much temptation for Annie," she always says. I was pretty sure she would say the same thing again, but I asked, just in case.

"Do you think we could stop and get some?" I asked very quietly.

"Sure," she said, surprising me. "We're not allergic, and besides, it's your day."

"Yippee!" I whooped.

"Yippee!" Mom whooped back.

We turned off the main road and down a small dirt path. For a minute, I was afraid Mom had taken a wrong turn. I was afraid we were going to drive into the middle of the field.

"Mom!" I cried.

Then I saw a small shack. A woman was standing behind a counter. It was heaped high with cartons of every size. Mom and I chose a medium-size one and walked to the end of a long row.

After a few minutes, we were both sitting on the damp ground, picking berries and laughing. They smelled sweet, and their juice came off on our hands and our clothes.

"It's been too long since I've seen you, my friend!" I said to a strawberry.

"You nut," said Mom, laughing.

On the way back to the shack, Mom said, "I hope they don't charge us extra."

"What do you mean?" I asked.

"Well, we do look like two giant strawberries," she said, teasing.

"You goof," I said.

Back in the car, the strawberries smelled delicious. We couldn't wait to taste them.

"Appetizers?" Mom asked, as she offered me a big, juicy one.

"I don't mind if I do," I said.

It was lunchtime when we pulled into Dolphin Bay.

"What beautiful blue water," said Mom.

"It looks purple to me," I said.

"Bluebonnet water," we both said, at almost the same time. Then we giggled.

"I can't wait to get my feet wet," I said. "Let's go for a walk on the beach now."

"Not yet," said Mom, with a serious look on her face. "You promised Aunt Claire we would visit Mrs. Ivey."

Around my house, a promise always comes first. We drove down a narrow gravel road. All along the road were houses that sat out over the water. They seemed to be standing on giant toothpicks.

"Let's see," said Mom, "Sis said her house is brown."

"Green, Mom," I said.

"Oops!" she said. "And it's the third on the right?"

"The fourth on the left," I answered.

"Really!" she said.

As we walked up the steps, I noticed that the paint on the house was peeling and that it looked like an old sea-battered boat. I hoped to myself that this visit wouldn't take long.

I peeked in through the screen door. The sound of sad music was coming from inside. Mom knocked once, and when no one answered, she knocked again. The music stopped. Then Mom called out, "Mrs. Ivey, I'm Claire's sister and this is my daughter, Sara. May we come in?"

"Certainly," said a gentle voice on the other side.

It was dark and musty-smelling inside. I stayed behind Mom, just in case. Then Mrs. Ivey pulled back the drapes, and sunlight flooded the room. I could see much better. There was a record player next to the chair and a round wooden table in the middle of the room. Mrs. Ivey's left foot was in a cast, and she was walking with a cane.

"Did you have any trouble finding my house?" she asked.

"I'm afraid I would never have found it, if it hadn't been for Sara," said Mom. "She has a good sense of direction."

While Mom and Mrs. Ivey talked, I looked around the room. There were no toys or games. There was nothing to do but look out the window.

"Sara, I think there's a soda in the refrigerator," said Mrs. Ivey. "Please help yourself."

Mom and I went into the kitchen. When I opened the refrigerator to get the soda, I noticed it looked empty like ours does after Annie and I have had a lot of friends over.

"I wish I could offer you lunch," Mrs. Ivey called from the other room, "but I haven't been to the store much since I hurt my ankle."

Mom and I took a quick glance around the kitchen. We have plenty of food in our basket, I thought to myself.

"Mrs. Ivey, why don't you share our picnic lunch with us?" I offered, surprising myself.

"Sara, that's a lovely idea," said Mom.

"I'd be delighted," said Mrs. Ivey. "We can eat on the dock, over the water."

I held the door open for Mrs. Ivey while Mom brought the picnic basket around. I was glad that I had made an extra sandwich.

When we were all sitting down, I opened the jar of olives and passed around the toothpicks.

"My, I didn't know I was being invited to such an elegant meal," said Mrs. Ivey, laughing.

Sea gulls hovered over our heads and begged for food. When I finished eating, I tossed them my crumbs. Then I walked to the edge of the dock. I kicked off my shoes and dangled my feet in the cool water.

Then Mom pulled off her shoes and sat next to me. We wiggled our toes back and forth and watched as sunlight danced in little ripples over our feet.

In the distance, I could see a dark line of clouds. It seemed to be moving toward us. I hoped the clouds weren't rain clouds. I hoped they would just disappear. But as we talked, the sky began to darken and the wind picked up. Soon, the little ripples of water turned into waves. They slapped against the dock. Then the rain began to pour down, out over the bay.

Quickly, I helped Mom gather up our things. Then I held the door for Mrs. Ivey. We were just back inside when the rain hit in big, splashy drops against the windowpanes. I felt sad.

"I'm afraid we won't get to walk on the beach now," I told Mom.

"I'm sure the rain will be over soon," she said.

Mom and Mrs. Ivey talked while I looked out the window, at the rain. Then Mom called me into the kitchen. She whispered, "Mrs. Ivey has asked me to get a few things for her at the grocery store. Would you mind staying here with her until I get back?"

"Well, all right," I whispered back. But secretly, I was thinking that this day was not turning out the way I had planned.

While Mom was gone, I stared out the window some more. There was nothing better to do. Mrs. Ivey must have noticed the look on my face, because she said, "Whenever I feel sad, I play music. There's nothing like music to chase the blues away."

She picked up an old, black case. It was worn and the edges were frayed. Inside was a beautiful clarinet with shiny silver keys.

"Would you like to try and play a note?" she asked.

"Me?" I asked. "Sure!"

She put her hands around mine and showed me how to hold the clarinet. It felt smooth and cool and wonderful, just the way I thought it would. Then she showed me how to put my mouth on it and blow. I tried, but no sound came out. I kept blowing, but still no sound came out. I began to feel dizzy.

"Easy does it," said Mrs. Ivey.

I tried again. This time a sound came out, softly at first, then building into a full deep note.

"Neat!" I cried.

"Wonderful," said Mrs. Ivey. "Now you've had your first clarinet lesson."

Carefully, I handed it back to her.

"Would you play something?" I asked.

"Sure," she said. "How about something snappy?"

She picked out a record and put it on her record-player. "I'll play along with this," she said.

The music started. Mrs. Ivey tapped her good foot, then lifted the clarinet to her mouth. The notes began to tumble out—high notes, low notes, and fast notes. I tapped my foot too. Then I clapped my hands. Before I knew it, I was dancing around the room.

"Go, Mrs. Ivey!" I shouted.

She took a breath. "Let's raise the roof!" she shouted back.

Her good foot was tapping wildly. I was spinning around the room. When the record ended, I collapsed into the chair, next to Mrs. Ivey. We were both laughing and out of breath. That's when I noticed Mom had come back.

"It looks like I missed quite a party," she said, smiling. She was holding a big bag of groceries.

"You sure did," we both said, at almost the same time. Then we laughed some more.

"Thank you so much for picking up my groceries," Mrs. Ivey said to Mom.

I could tell by the look on Mrs. Ivey's face that she was pleased.

I helped Mom put the groceries away. Suddenly, the refrigerator looked normal again.

Then I put a pot of water on the stove to heat.

"What are you up to?" asked Mom.

"You'll see," I said.

I ran out to the car and grabbed the carton of strawberries.

We had tea and strawberries and talked about the weather, just the three of us.

"I believe the rain is over," said Mrs. Ivey.

"We'd better hurry if we want to take that walk along the beach," Mom told me.

"Sara, I hope you'll come back and visit," said Mrs. Ivey. "I'd love to give you another lesson."

I leaned over and gave her a hug. "Next time I'll bring my sister, Annie. She plays the flute," I said. "Then we'll really raise the roof!"

"I'd like that," Mrs. Ivey said, smiling.

Mom and I took a long walk on the beach. The sun was twinkling on the dark water and turning it golden. I put my short hand into Mom's long, slender one. I felt happy and proud to be with her. After a while, I said, "We'd better go now."

"Whatever you say, Sara," said Mom. "It's your day."

On the drive home, Mom and I stopped by the field of wildflowers. I picked a bunch of bluebonnets. It's funny, I thought, but I can't wait to share my day with Annie.